AR 2.5

Mc D   M   books:

First series

Second series

LEEDS CITY COLLEGE
PARK LANE CAMPUS LRC
R 66 505

Dark Man

The Dark Waters of Time
by Peter Lancett
illustrated by Jan Pedroietta

Published by Ransom Publishing Ltd.
51 Southgate Street, Winchester, Hampshire SO23 9EH
www.ransom.co.uk

ISBN   978 184167 413 1

First published in 2006
Second printing 2008

Copyright © 2006 Ransom Publishing Ltd.

Text copyright © 2006 Peter Lancett
Illustrations copyright © 2006 Jan Pedroietta

A CIP catalogue record of this book is available from the British Library.

The rights of Peter Lancett to be identified as the author and of Jan Pedroietta to be identified as the illustrator of this Work have been asserted by them in accordance with sections 77 and 78 of the Copyright, Design and Patents Act 1988.

David Strachan, The Old Man, and The Shadow Masters appear by kind permission of Peter Lancett.

Printed in China through Colorcraft Ltd., Hong Kong.

Dark Man

The Dark Waters of Time

by Peter Lancett

illustrated by Jan Pedroietta

Park Lane College

R66505

Chapter One:
Murder in her Soul

"Protect her, but watch her," the Old Man had said.

The Dark Man knows that the girl has power.

He is leading her into the bad part of the city.

He sees her stare at people that they pass on the streets.

The girl is called Angela but she is no angel.

He sees that she has murder in her soul.

Yet Angela has a gift, so they must use her.

Chapter Two:
In the Secret Place

Here, in the bad part of the city, there is a secret place.

Under the ground is a pool of magical water.

The Dark Man pulls Angela into a doorway.

The building is in ruins, but they step inside.

The Dark Man knows a secret way,
below the ground.

They walk along black tunnels, where
the air is hot and steamy.

From around a corner, they hear voices.

The Dark Man goes ahead.

They might be demons, sent by the
Shadow Masters.

Then he finds them, five teenage boys.

They are afraid when they see him.

"Get out of here," the Dark Man tells them.

As they rush to get past him, Angela grabs one boy by the throat.

The Dark Man pulls her hand away.

"No," he says, and the boy runs away.

Chapter Three:
The Chamber of Shadows

A few minutes later they are standing in a chamber of shadows.

This is where the Dark Waters of Time are.

Angela can look into the water and see the past.

The waters will show her where the Golden Cup was last hidden.

Angela places her hands into the water and stares.

The Dark Man has to look away, the water will drive him insane.

Angela screams and falls back from the water.

The Dark Man holds her.

Her eyes are wild with fear.

"You must seek it where the iron melts," she gasps.

She will not say more, so the Dark Man leads them back to the streets.

Chapter Four:
As the Wind Blows

Across the road they see the boys.

The Dark Man notices Angela looking at them.

He knows what she wants to do.

He looks away, to the smart part of the city.

When he turns back, Angela has gone.

So have the boys.

As the wind blows around him, he hears a scream.

He knows that Angela is among the boys, but he cannot care.

He has got what he came for.

The author

photograph: Rachel Ottewill

Peter Lancett used to work in the movies. Then he worked in the city. Now he writes horror stories for a living. "It beats having a proper job," he says.

R66505